JOKE SHOP

TIM COLLINS

Badger
LEARNING

Joke Shop ISBN 978-1-78147-957-5

Text © Tim Collins 2014
Complete work © Badger Publishing Limited 2014

Publisher: Susan Ross
Senior Editor: Danny Pearson
Publishing Assistant: Claire Morgan
Copyeditor: Cheryl Lanyon
Designer: Bigtop Design Ltd

2 4 6 8 10 9 7 5 3 1

JOKE SHOP

Titles in Teen Reads:

Badger Publishing Limited, Oldmedow Road, Hardwick Industrial Estate, King's Lynn PE30 4JJ
Telephone: 01438 791037

www.badgerlearning.co.uk

CHAPTER 1

THE CHATTERING TEETH

"Have you heard about Andrea's fart, Aaron?" asked Jack.

"Only about twenty times," I said.

Andrea Taylor, one of the best-looking girls in year eleven had farted in class. But that wasn't all. The fart in question had gone on and on and on.

It had continued as she darted out of the classroom with her face turning deep red and had echoed as she ran down the corridor. She had gone home sick and, for all we knew, the record-breaking fart might still be going on.

"Ryan Brooks did it," said Jack. "He put fart powder in her Ribena."

I was surprised it had worked. I remember trying to put some in my babysitter's tea when I was eight. I watched her from behind a cushion on our living-room chair, but nothing happened.

Jack was sitting opposite Natasha and me in the school cafeteria. He had greasy, black hair and streaks of acne on his cheeks. He was clutching a stripy paper bag with the words 'Joke Shop' printed in large, black letters.

"He got it from here," he said, tapping the bag. "Just opened in the precinct. Want to see what I got?"

"Not really," I said. "But go ahead."

He emptied the bag onto the table. There was a pair of chattering teeth, a fake dog poo and a packet of blue-mouth sweets. There was an illustration on these of a boy sticking his blue tongue out.

Jack wound the chattering teeth and sent them across the table to me. I wasn't sure what was meant to be so hilarious about a set of teeth and gums that hopped along on flat, pink feet.

He opened the bag of blue-mouth sweets and held them out to a passing group of year seven pupils. A small boy called Patrick grabbed one and popped it in his mouth.

Jack giggled.

"Very mature," said Natasha, who was sitting next to me. She pulled her hair back and fixed a band around it.

"So's this," said Jack. He threw the dog poo and it landed on her empty plate. She leaped from her chair, scraping its legs across the floor with a loud screech.

"It's just a fake one," said Jack. "Look."

He leaned over and poked the turd with his finger. His face fell and he drew his hand back.

Jack had left a small, round dent in the poo. Rather than shiny and plastic it was now slimy and fresh. A bitter, disgusting smell was coming from it that hit the back of my throat and made me feel like throwing up.

Jack winced and wiped his finger on the empty paper bag.

"You are so nasty," spluttered Natasha. She pulled her jumper up over her nose.

There was a scream from the other side of the canteen. Patrick was holding his hand over his lips while blue liquid gushed out from between his fingers. He sobbed, glugging more onto the floor.

I felt a sharp stabbing in my fingers and looked down.

The chattering teeth had made their way over to me. They'd left a deep bite-mark across the side of my index finger and broken the skin just below my nail.

Blood was slowly trickling out.

CHAPTER 2

THE SNAKE

Our headmaster, Mr Davies, was standing at the front of the hall with his arms crossed.

"What has got into you lot?" he asked. "In the past week alone, I've had pupils sent to me for bringing in cigarettes, putting flies in drinks and even leaving dead chickens lying around."

I knew what had got into them all. Fake cigarettes, plastic flies and rubber chickens were all things you could buy from a joke shop. Whatever was happening in the school, it was all coming from that new shop in the precinct. I decided to check it out.

"From now on, anyone caught disrupting lessons will be suspended," said Mr Davies. "And I'm cancelling fancy-dress day for Halloween. You can still give a pound to charity if you like, but school uniform must be worn."

I could hear tutting and muttering coming from all around me.

"I've already got my costume," a girl called Megan whispered in the row behind me. "I'm wearing it whatever he says."

A girl with long, blond hair at the front of the hall stuck her hand up.

"What is it?" asked Mr Davies.

"There's a spider, sir!" said the girl. A large, black shape was scuttling over the floor in front of her.

"I hardly think it's going to harm you," said Mr Davies.

I wasn't so sure. I only caught a glimpse of it as it rushed for the curtain at the back of the hall, but it looked pretty massive. More like a tarantula than a normal spider.

"Ryan Brooks sent it at me," said the girl. "He keeps doing it."

Mr Davies pointed at Ryan Brooks, who was sitting behind the girl.

"Stand up!" he shouted.

Ryan got to his feet. He was a small, year ten pupil with short, brown hair and a blazer that was too large for him. His face was red and he was shuffling around awkwardly.

"What is that?" asked Mr Davies.

He pointed at Ryan's blazer. The right side was wiggling around on its own.

Ryan reached into his jacket and took out a writhing snake. It had yellow and black stripes and a forked tongue that was darting in and out.

All around the hall, pupils jumped to their feet. A few of them ran for the door and tried to crowd through it at the same time.

"Stay where you are!" shouted Mr Davies. "I'll dismiss you one form at a time."

More pupils got up and crushed around the exit. I spotted a tall boy pushing a year seven boy aside as he ran. The boy crashed to the floor and rolled around with his hands on his knee.

"Keep calm!" shouted Mr Davies. "And someone call the RSPCA. We need to take care of that thing."

Ryan was still standing at the front of the hall, holding the snake below its head while its body coiled around his arm.

"It was rubber," he said. "I swear it was rubber."

CHAPTER 3

THE SHOP

We climbed the rusty wheelchair ramp that curved up from the street to the precinct. We walked past the newsagent and the empty shop that used to sell CDs, and turned the corner.

You couldn't miss it.

It was in the place where the old video rental store had been. A large, yellow sign above the window had the words 'Joke Shop' and a painting of a grinning jester in a pink and green costume.

Fake vomit, rubber chickens and plastic spiders were jumbled in the window. In the centre was a clown mask with tufts of green hair and black diamonds painted around its empty eyeholes. I think it was meant to be grinning, but the bottom half of it was sagging in a way that made it look sad.

Neon signs with the words 'LAUGHS', 'SHOCKS' and 'SCREAMS' had been stuck inside the window.

"Ugh, look at that Aaron. Nasty!" said Natasha, pointing at the clown. "I hope I don't meet him on the way home tonight."

I pushed the door open and a bell rang. The wooden shelves on the sides of the shop were lined with whoopee cushions, plastic insects and trick soap. Everything seemed to be covered in a thick layer of dust. Hadn't this place just opened?

A row of costumes hung down the middle of the shop. There were vampires, witches, werewolves, ninjas, pirates and a baggy, white body-suit with orange pompoms that must have been part of the clown outfit.

I had to walk past the dangling costumes to see the counter.

An old man was standing behind a glass case full of plastic snakes, bats and spiders. An old-fashioned, wooden cash register was perched next to him, displaying the price '14p'.

"Can I help you?" asked the man, leaning forwards and smiling. He had thinning, grey hair and was wearing a white shirt and beige cardigan.

"We're just browsing," said Natasha.

The old man reached into his counter and pulled out a white packet with 'FART POWDER' written on it. "Can I interest you in this? Guaranteed to raise a smile."

He blew a raspberry and wafted his hand in front of his nose.

"My friend already used some," I said. "Apparently it worked a little too well. So have a lot of the tricks you sell. Why is that?"

A frown flickered across the old man's mouth, but it soon lifted back into a smile.

"I understand," he said. "You want a gag of your own. Something they haven't seen before."

He tapped a plastic jar next to the till. "Exploding sweets. You won't believe the stir these will cause. Perfect for Halloween."

I remembered Patrick clutching his mouth as the liquid poured out. If that's what the blue-mouth sweets did, what would these do? Blow someone's jaw off?

Natasha shook her head. "Thanks, but no thanks."

"I've got it," said the man. He reached into his counter and pulled out a brown packet with 'ITCHING POWDER' written on it.

I imagined Patrick scratching the side of his face until it was red and sore. It was a pitiful and painful image, but for a split second I also found it incredibly funny. I realised I was grinning.

"No," I said, forcing the smile away.

I wanted to keep asking him about why his tricks had been causing such chaos. We'd come here to confront him, not to browse. But my mind was getting fuzzy.

"Your jokes have been hurting people," said Natasha. "We think they're dangerous."

At least she'd managed to hold it together.

"I've got it!" said the old man.

He pulled a rubber finger out of his glass counter. Red blood had been painted over the stump and there was a scrap of squishy, white bone sticking out of the end.

"Imagine putting this in your teacher's coffee," said the old man. "He'd get a shock, wouldn't he?"

The man began to laugh and I found myself joining in. I turned to Natasha and saw she was chuckling along too.

I imagined my history teacher, Mr Singh, fishing it out of his mug and it seemed like the most hilarious thing I'd ever thought of. I was laughing so hard I had to wipe tears from the corners of my eyes.

"One pound, twenty two," said the old man through his chuckles. I scooped out all the coins in my pocket and clacked them down on the counter. It turned out I had exactly the right amount.

"Perfect!" said the old man. He placed the rubber finger in a stripy paper bag and handed it over. "Come again!"

"Thanks!" said Natasha.

We were both still laughing as we circled down the wheelchair ramp, but our giggles dried up as we continued along the street. By the time we'd reached the bus stop, I was starting to wonder what I'd found so funny. So what if Mr Singh found a rubber finger in his coffee?

I glanced at Natasha. She wasn't laughing either. In fact, she looked pretty freaked out. She was glaring at the paper bag.

I looked down at it. Dark red liquid was dripping from the corner. I peered inside. The finger was no longer made of rubber. It was pale, dead flesh. There was a genuine shard of snapped bone sticking out of it, and the liquid dripping from it wasn't red paint. It was blood.

CHAPTER 4

HALLOWEEN

Jack grinned, showing off his plastic fangs.

It was Halloween and a small group of pupils had turned up in fancy dress, ignoring the headmaster's ban.

There were three in our class, sitting around the back table. Jack was dressed as a vampire, Liam was dressed as a werewolf, and Megan was dressed as a witch.

Mr Singh shoved his thick, black glasses up the bridge of his nose, opened his laptop and pointed at the chunk of text on the whiteboard.

"Quiet," he said. "Read this source carefully, as I'm about to ask you some questions about it."

A low murmur of chat continued.

Mr Singh lifted his finger to his lips and said, "Shush!"

Megan stood up. She was wearing a pointed, black hat and had a long, warty, rubber nose attached by elastic.

"Silence!" she shouted, waving a plastic wand.

Laughter broke out.

"I don't think that helped, Megan," said Mr Singh. "Now settle down and read the source."

"I can't concentrate," shouted a girl called Alison Green. "Liam keeps growling."

There was more laughter as the whole class turned to look at the back table. Liam was staring down at his desk and I could only see the long snout and furry ears of his mask.

"Cut it out," said Mr Singh.

Alison was right about him growling. We could all hear it now.

"Come on Liam," sighed Mr Singh. "Don't make me send you to Mr Davies."

The growl got deeper and louder.

Alison stormed over to Liam's desk and pointed at him. "Shut up!" she shouted. "That's getting on my nerves!"

Liam looked up. His eyes were yellow with long, black pupils. I wondered if the costume had come with special contact lenses.

He snarled and lashed out at Alison, scratching three red lines down her cheek. She shrieked and rubbed them with her palm.

"Look what he did," cried Alison, pointing to her cheek. "Expel him."

"Get out now!" shouted Mr Singh in an uneven voice. He pointed at the door. "Report to Mr Davies!"

Liam fixed his yellow eyes on him and howled.

"Out!" shouted Mr Singh. But his hands were beginning to tremble.

"If you won't do anything about him, I will," said Alison. She walked around the desk, but Jack bolted up and blocked her path.

"Move!" shouted Alison.

Jack grabbed her shoulders and thrust his plastic fangs into her neck. He pulled back and there were small drops of blood on the ends of them. Except they didn't seem plastic any more. They looked like genuine, sharp teeth.

"All three of you get out!" shouted Mr Singh. There were beads of sweat rolling down his cheeks and his glasses were slipping down his nose. "Right now!"

Megan stood up. She grinned, pointed her wand at him and shouted, "Silence!"

Mr Singh's lips kept moving but no sound came out. He grabbed his throat and silently opened and closed his mouth like a fish.

Liam, Megan and Jack burst out laughing.

CHAPTER 5

THE OLD MAN IS A LIAR

Natasha nudged me and pointed to a boy called Lewis, who was lurching around the canteen dressed as Frankenstein's monster. He was wearing a mask with sunken eyes and green skin. At least, I'd assumed it was a mask. It looked more like brilliant movie make-up now I was staring right at him.

"See that idiot, Aaron? He just ruined our science lesson," said Natasha. "He kept knocking beakers off the desks and smashing them on the floor."

Lewis lumbered into a table and a can of Fanta fell off.

"Our history lesson was even weirder thanks to that lot," I said. I pointed at Liam, Jack and Megan, who were sitting at the other end of the lunch hall. Megan's nose was staying on without any elastic now, Jack's skin had faded to white, and Liam was eating straight from his plate.

"That costume lot have gone weird," said Natasha. She pointed at a boy in a ninja costume who was stalking across the hall. He flipped over backwards, kicking a plate of chicken curry and rice out of a small boy's hand and sending it spinning into the air.

He landed gracefully while the plate crashed down behind him.

"We need to stop it," said Natasha.

"I don't fancy taking them on," I said. "My Kung Fu's a little rusty."

I heard a scraping noise from the other side of the canteen. A girl dressed as a pirate was dragging a metal hook along the wall and ripping a white line in the plaster. The plastic parrot on her shoulder fluttered into life and flew up to the ceiling.

"I mean we need to go back to the shop," said Natasha. "That's where they've been getting these costumes from. And why they're all acting so weirdly."

I thought about the rubber finger and how hilarious it had seemed when we'd bought it.

"Something happens when you go in," I said. "It's like a spell takes over and you can't see how bad it all is. What if that happens to us again?"

Liam was shoving his plate away with his muzzle. He threw his head back and howled, showing off a row of razor-sharp teeth.

"It won't," said Natasha. "Because we'll be expecting it this time."

She took a ballpoint pen out of her pocket, pulled my palm towards her and scrawled:

The old man is a liar and his tricks are evil.

"There you go," she said. "Look at that if you're having trouble."

Over on the other side of the hall, Megan was strolling past a table full of year seven girls. She waved her wand and muttered. Their plates all flipped over at once, coating their shirts with vegetable pasta, beans, gravy and custard.

"Come on," said Natasha. "We've got to do something about this before it gets out of control."

CHAPTER 6

THE CLOWN MASK

The bell rang as we walked into the shop. The old man was stacking coins on his counter. Some were rusty and faded, as if they'd been dug out of an ancient site.

"How did the trick go?" he asked. "I bet your teacher's face was a picture, wasn't it?"

I'd rehearsed loads of stuff to say but I couldn't remember any of it now.

"We didn't use it," said Natasha. "We want you to stop selling your crooked stuff to everyone from our school."

The old man's face fell and he shook his head.

"Well that is a shame," he said. "It upsets me so much when my customers aren't satisfied. Let me make it up to you with a free gift."

He pulled a plastic flower with a small pump attachment out of the glass counter.

"Everyone loves a squirting flower," he said. "And this is the best you've ever seen. It's so powerful it'll take their eyes out."

I thought about blasting Liam, Megan and Jack with a painful jet of water. That would teach them to parade around with their silly costumes on.

I felt the sides of my mouth lifting into a smile.

The old man offered the flower to Natasha and she turned it over in her hands. She was grinning, too.

I looked at the words she'd scrawled on my palm:

The old man is a liar and his tricks are evil.

The fog cleared from my mind. I grabbed the plastic flower and threw it over the counter.

"We don't want the stupid thing," I said. "We just want you to stop selling stuff to our school. Someone's going to get killed."

"At least they'll die with a smile on their face," said the old man. "There's nothing wrong with a good, old-fashioned chuckle."

"There *is* something wrong," said Natasha. She was frowning again now, and had her eyes fixed on the old man. "This whole thing is wrong and we want you to stop."

"Or you'll do what?" asked the old man.

"Call the police," I said.

"And they'll walk out of here with bags of fart powder and chattering teeth," he said, "thinking about all the hilarious tricks they're going to play back at the station."

"Then maybe we'll take matters into our own hands," said Natasha.

The old man grinned. "You'd beat up a weak, old man just because you don't like his shop? Now that's something the police would be interested in."

He had a point. And it's not like I'd have carried out Natasha's threats anyway. I've never had a fight in my life. Besides, he only wanted to make people laugh. Why did we want to punish him for that?

No. That wasn't right.

My thoughts were getting blurry again so I tried to look at the words on my hand:

The old man is a joker and his tricks are hilarious.

I was certain that wasn't what Natasha
had written.

I was still puzzling over it when the old man
grabbed something out of his case and held it
out to me.

It was a scrap of white rubber with black
diamonds and flashes of green.

The clown mask. The one that had been at the
centre of the window display.

I started to giggle. What a funny clown he
was. I could imagine him tumbling and falling
and leaping and prancing… and biting and
scratching.

"Isn't it magnificent?" asked the old man. "The
finest in the shop. Can you believe no one's rented
it out yet? On this most special of days, too."

He lifted a baggy, white costume from under the
counter. It had a wide, lace collar and a row of

red pompoms up the middle. He put it on the counter and placed a foam custard pie next to it.

"The whole costume's still here," he said. He looked down at it and then up at me. "I've just thought of something. Why don't you borrow it? It might stop you feeling so grumpy."

I imagined myself leaping out from behind a corner and shoving the custard pie into the face of one of those year seven brats. I sniggered. The more they begged me to stop, the harder I'd shove it into their snivelling noses.

I found myself laughing again. A voice in the back of my mind was trying to tell me this wouldn't be funny at all. It would be horrific.

I ignored it and gave in to childish glee. I felt like I was eight again, sniggering behind the cushion and waiting for the fart powder to work on my babysitter.

That hadn't worked. But this would. The tricks from this shop always worked and they always made people scream.

Natasha turned and wandered down the row of costumes lining the middle of the shop.

"You can take any you like, young lady," said the man. "If you've ever wanted to feel sharp fangs in your mouth or strong claws sprouting from your fingertips, this is your chance. Don't be shy."

He clasped his hands together and gasped. "I know what you've seen. It's the jester costume, isn't it? Oh, how wonderful. Imagine all the mischief a clown and a jester could get up to on Halloween."

Natasha wandered round to the other side of the costumes and I couldn't see her any more. The voice in my mind spoke up again. It said this was all going wrong, that Natasha had fallen under his spell and that it was all up to me now.

The voice told me to try reading the words on my hand again.

I lifted my palm to my face:

The old man is your friend, so put the clown costume on and make them all scream like the little pigs they are.

My head was swimming. That couldn't be right. There was no way the words on my hand could say all that.

As I thought about it, I found myself stepping into the bulky, white costume. I didn't even remember taking it off the counter.

"And now for the most important bit," said the old man.

He handed me the mask.

The voice in my head told me to throw it to the ground and stamp on it. That if I put it on it wouldn't even be a mask any more. I'd touch my face and find it was covered in white make-up.

Then I'd be the happy clown and I'd dance back into school and tumble and fall and leap and prance... and kill and kill and kill.

I could hear the costumes rustling behind me.

"What have you chosen, young lady?" asked the old man, peering down the row. "I bet it was the jester, wasn't it?"

"No," said Natasha. "I've found a much, much better one."

She stepped back into view. She was wearing a black robe with a hood that covered her face, and carrying a long, wooden stick with a curved blade.

"Death itself," said the old man. "The Grim Reaper. An excellent choice. Just think of all the fun you can have with that on Halloween. Where will you even begin?"

"Right here," said Natasha.

She ran towards the counter with her finger stretched out. The old man's eyes widened and he pushed himself against the back wall. He was trembling, and his thin, grey hair was flopping down over his forehead.

"Stop!" he shouted. "Get away from me! Get out of my shop!"

Natasha leaned forwards and tapped his chest.

The old man screamed and collapsed to the floor as the lights flickered out.

CHAPTER 7

THE EMPTY SHOP

As my eyes adjusted to the gloom, I noticed the inside of the shop looked very different.

Instead of wooden shelves lining the wall, I could see the old plastic racks of the video rental shop. They were stuffed with empty drink cans and faded crisp packets instead of fart powder and chattering teeth. There was a high counter at the end of the room and the old-fashioned till was gone.

The mask I'd been holding had vanished, too. It seemed impossible that I'd had anything in my hands just a split second ago.

My clown costume was covered in dark stains. The pompoms were missing and the sleeves were ripped into narrow strips. It reeked of stagnant water as I stepped out of it and kicked it across the dusty floor.

Natasha's robe was spotted with white patches of mould. She threw it aside and wiped her hands on her shirt.

"Do you think he's really dead?" I asked, looking over at the counter.

"I'm not sure he was ever really alive," said Natasha.

She tiptoed over to the counter and I followed, convinced the old man was about to leap up and cover us with itching powder.

There was nothing on the other side but a coffee-stained carpet. The old man had gone.

*

The chaos in the canteen was over by the time we got back. There were just a few year seven pupils cleaning the walls and tables with wet cloths.

I spotted Patrick, the boy who'd eaten the blue-mouth sweet. He was dragging a sponge across the yellow surface of a table.

"What happened?" I asked.

"Jack and the others are going to get expelled," he said. "For what they did."

"Why are they making you lot clean up?" asked Natasha.

Patrick shrugged. "Mr Davies said we're all to blame for getting carried away and making up stories. I don't really care, though. I know what happened to me."

He pulled his collar back to reveal two small bite marks.

We never saw Jack, Megan, Liam or any of

the other costume wearers again. Whenever anyone spoke about them, they never mentioned vampires or werewolves or witches. It was always 'practical jokes that got out of hand', or 'pranks that went too far'.

At the next assembly, Mr Davies announced that the school would never be celebrating Halloween again. This seemed to settle the matter, as if it had all been nothing more than a few pupils in fancy dress getting overexcited.

Nobody seemed to speak about the joke shop as time went on. I chatted to Natasha about it a few times, but we both had very hazy memories. It was as if we were remembering something from years, rather than weeks, ago.

But something just happened that brought it all back. I'm sitting on a fast train that's speeding through hundreds of little stations I can't read the names of. A few minutes ago, I glanced up a street and spotted a bright yellow shop.

I only saw it for half a second, but there was no mistaking it. There was a picture of a grinning jester above it, and I'm sure I saw the green hair and black diamond eyes of a clown mask in the window.

Maybe it was just a coincidence that someone has opened a joke shop and chosen exactly the same sign and window display. I hope so. But if I lived in that town, I'd steer very clear of anyone dressed as a vampire, witch or clown.

Especially tomorrow.

Tomorrow is Halloween.

THE END